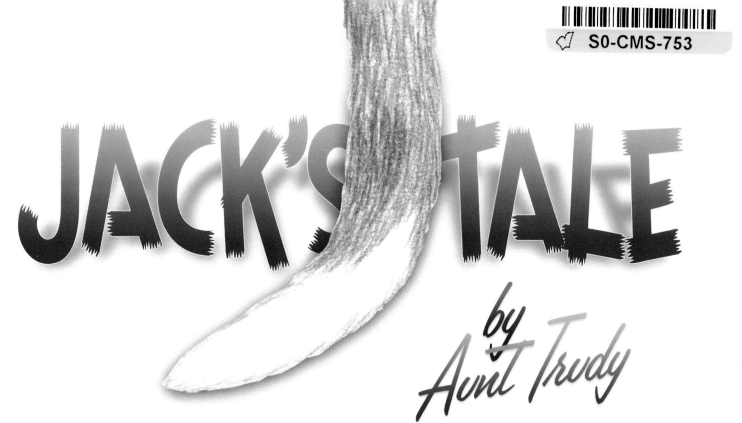

JACK'S TALE

by
Aunt Trudy

ISBN: 1-4196-5499-3
ISBN-13: 9781419654992

Visit www.booksurge.com to order additional copies

DEDICATED TO BILL
AND THE DREAM

Jack loved being with his brothers and sisters.

All together there were five of them; with Jack, six. They would tease him and try to wrestle with him until he would jump on their back or on top of the table and swat at them as they ran under the table.

Momma Ellie would growl at him to mind his manners but she was soft where Jack was concerned and everyone knew it. She didn't have favorites but if she did, they all knew it would have to be Jack because after all she did save his life…

4

It was a month or two ago when Master brought home a little, ragged, wet bundle of fur and her heart went out to the little one who looked so lost. Master put the thing on the floor and went to get it some milk and when he returned he found Jack snuggled into the soft fur on Momma Ellie's tummy. Jack was noisily drinking Ellie's milk right along with her own pups!

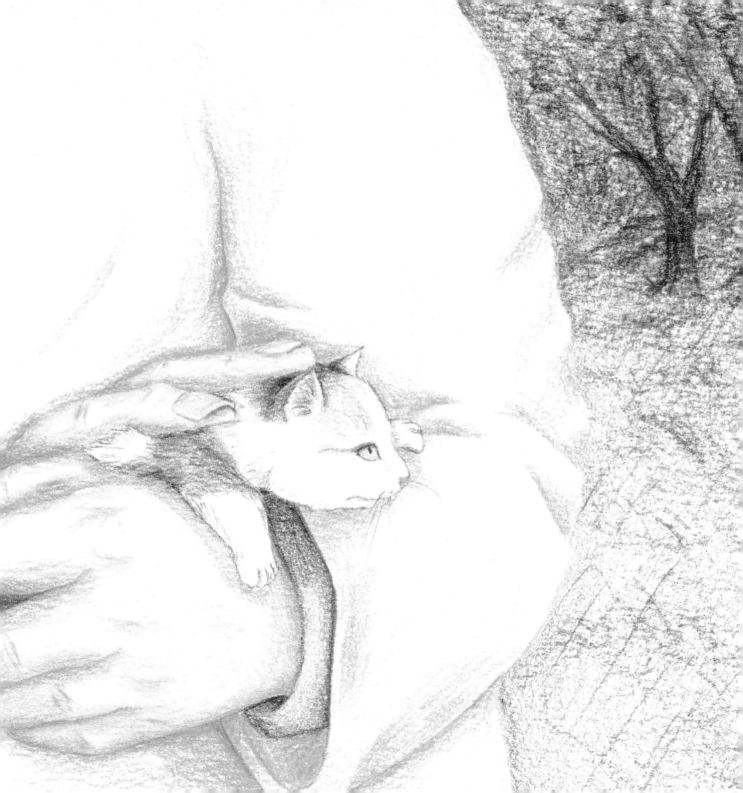

Since everyone seemed happy with this and Jack began to grow, the Master let it be. He figured soon enough Jack would grow into his own and be the cat he was meant to be!

To tell the truth, it never occurred to Jack or his brother and sister pups that he was anything different than they were. He was spotted and so were they. He had 2 ears and 4 feet and so did they. He had the love and protection of Momma Ellie and so did they.

They could all run and tumble together although Jack did do a lot more jumping than his brothers and sisters. They were all very interested in exploring the world just outside of Momma Ellie's tummy although they were quick to return to her for comfort and milk or just reassurance.

And they all had tails!

But as they grew, it became clear to Jack there was one difference…

They could make their tails move when they were happy and he couldn't.

As he watched, they could make their tail move up and down, back and forth and even in circles! How did they do that, he wondered… he did try but couldn't seem to make his tail do any of those wonderful things. Now he had a nice tail – a big bushy kind of tail. Truthfully, it seemed too large for him and when he sat down, he would often need to make a circle to make sure it wrapped around his paws and didn't stick out where it could get stepped on. He could make it stand upright, and sometimes the tip would kind of wiggle slowly like a bag of worms was inside.

12

But that wasn't something he could control like the other puppies seemed to be able to do with their tails. At first it didn't worry him too much but as time went by, he would practice trying to move his tail like they did. He would scrunch up his face and put all his energy into his tail but it did nothing!

It wouldn't move up or down, or back or forth, much less in circles! The harder he tried, the more he worried about it. And, the truth be told, the other puppies began to poke fun at his efforts and his tail that wouldn't wag.

14

They would sometimes giggle behind his back at his efforts – mostly because his face looked so funny when he tried so hard!

Now Momma Ellie was watching all this and felt sad for Jack when she saw how hard he was trying to make his tail do something it couldn't ever do. She knew all the time that Jack was not a puppy but, after all the difference between cats and dogs, kitties and puppies was not so great.

16

They were the same in many ways, especially when they were little ones. They got hungry and sucked milk the same. They all loved to tumble and run and explore the world at hand and run back to snuggle under her furry tummy when they had tired. She always felt that everyone made too much of the differences and not enough of the similarities and that in some ways, their futures were labeled by their differences rather than the similarities.

She had heard that was the way with humans as well. They judged each other, she had heard, by the differences between themselves like color of their 'fur' or eyes, or what sounds came from their tongues when they spoke , or even what they did or where they lived. The whole thing seemed very silly to Momma Ellie but, she had heard that humans take these things very seriously.

She really didn't want her little family to get caught up in these silly things so one day she decided it was time to chat with Jack. She picked a time when the other pups were caught up chasing after their shadows and Jack was busy trying to make his tail do what it couldn't. She nuzzled him fondly and he lost interest in his tail and began his funny throat noises. It always happened when he was particularly happy or contented and it sounded a bit like a honey bee with a sore throat!

Momma Ellie loved hearing the noise because she knew that all was well with Jack's little world when she heard that hum. Jack himself didn't really think anything about it so Momma Ellie pointed it out for him, and told him that he only made that noise when he was so happy he couldn't speak.

'You don't need to wag a tail' she told him,' to let everyone know when you are happy'! None of the other puppies could make that happy sound , she told him and Jack knew that to be so. He had never thought about it but it was the truth!

24

This was his special thing – the thing that he alone could do. Seen like this, not being able to move your tail suddenly seemed less important!

'Everyone is special in their own way, Momma Ellie told him, and this is your special thing! '

And Jack was so happy that the noise in his throat got louder and louder until neither he nor Momma Ellie could hear anything else!

THE END